SABAN'S
MIGHTY MORPHIN POWER RANGERS

9

WRITTEN BY
KYLE HIGGINS
ILLUSTRATED BY
HENDRY PRASETYA

COLORS BY
MATT HERMS
LETTERS BY
ED DUKESHIRE

COVER BY
JAMAL CAMPBELL
DESIGNER
JILLIAN CRAB
ASSISTANT EDITOR
MATTHEW LEVINE
ASSOCIATE EDITOR
ALEX GALER
EDITOR
DAFNA PLEBAN

HASBRO SPECIAL THANKS
BRIAN CASENTINI, MELISSA FLORES, EDGAR PASTEN, PAUL STRICKLAND, MARCY GEORGE, JASON BISCHOFF, ED LANE, BETH ARTALE, AND **MICHAEL KELLY**

ABDO Spotlight
BOOM! STUDIOS
Licensed by: Hasbro

ABDOBOOKS.COM

Reinforced library bound edition published in 2020 by Spotlight, a division of ABDO, PO Box 398166, Minneapolis, Minnesota 55439. Spotlight produces high-quality reinforced library bound editions for schools and libraries. Published by agreement with BOOM! Studios.

Printed in the United States of America, North Mankato, Minnesota.
092019
012020

THIS BOOK CONTAINS RECYCLED MATERIALS

Licensed by:

Library of Congress Control Number: 2019942386

Publisher's Cataloging-in-Publication Data

Names: Higgins, Kyle, author. | Prasetya, Hendry; Herms, Matt; Silas, Thony; Valenza, Bryan; illustrators.
Title: Mighty morphin power rangers/ writer: Kyle Higgins; art: Hendry Prasetya; Matt Herms; Thony Silas; Bryan Valenza.
Description: Minneapolis, Minnesota: Spotlight, 2020 | Series: Mighty morphin power rangers
Summary: Tommy Oliver was new in town when evil doer, Rita Repulsa, made him the Green Ranger. After escaping her mind control, he hopes for a normal life, which isn't easy to do with the plights of high school, making new friends, and the dangers that come with being a Power Ranger.
Identifiers: ISBN 9781532144233 (#1, lib. bdg.) | ISBN 9781532144240 (#2, lib. bdg.) | ISBN 9781532144257 (#3, lib. bdg.) | ISBN 9781532144264 (#4, lib. bdg.) | ISBN 9781532144271 (#5, lib. bdg.) | ISBN 9781532144288 (#6, lib. bdg.) | ISBN 9781532144295 (#7, lib. bdg.) | ISBN 9781532144301 (#8, lib. bdg.) | ISBN 9781532144318 (#9, lib. bdg.)
Subjects: LCSH: Mighty Morphin Power Rangers (Television program)--Juvenile fiction. | Ninjas--Juvenile fiction. | Superheroes--Juvenile fiction. | Good and evil--Juvenile fiction. | Graphic novels--Juvenile fiction. | Comic books, strips, etc.--Juvenile fiction
Classification: DDC 741.5--dc23

Spotlight

A Division of ABDO
abdobooks.com

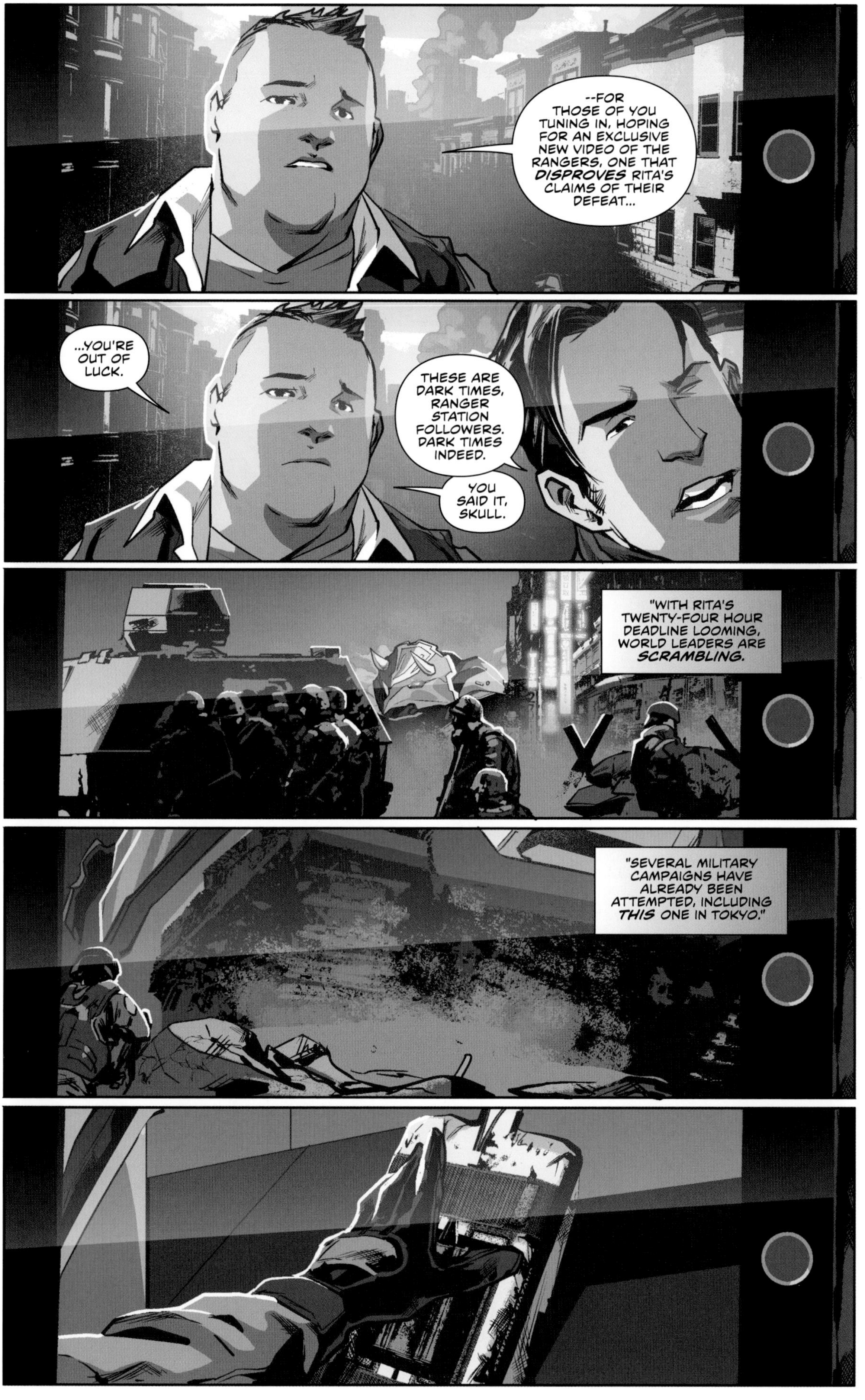
--FOR THOSE OF YOU TUNING IN, HOPING FOR AN EXCLUSIVE NEW VIDEO OF THE RANGERS, ONE THAT *DISPROVES* RITA'S CLAIMS OF THEIR DEFEAT...
...YOU'RE OUT OF LUCK.
THESE ARE DARK TIMES, RANGER STATION FOLLOWERS. DARK TIMES INDEED.
YOU SAID IT, SKULL.
"WITH RITA'S TWENTY-FOUR HOUR DEADLINE LOOMING, WORLD LEADERS ARE *SCRAMBLING.*
"SEVERAL MILITARY CAMPAIGNS HAVE ALREADY BEEN ATTEMPTED, INCLUDING *THIS* ONE IN TOKYO."

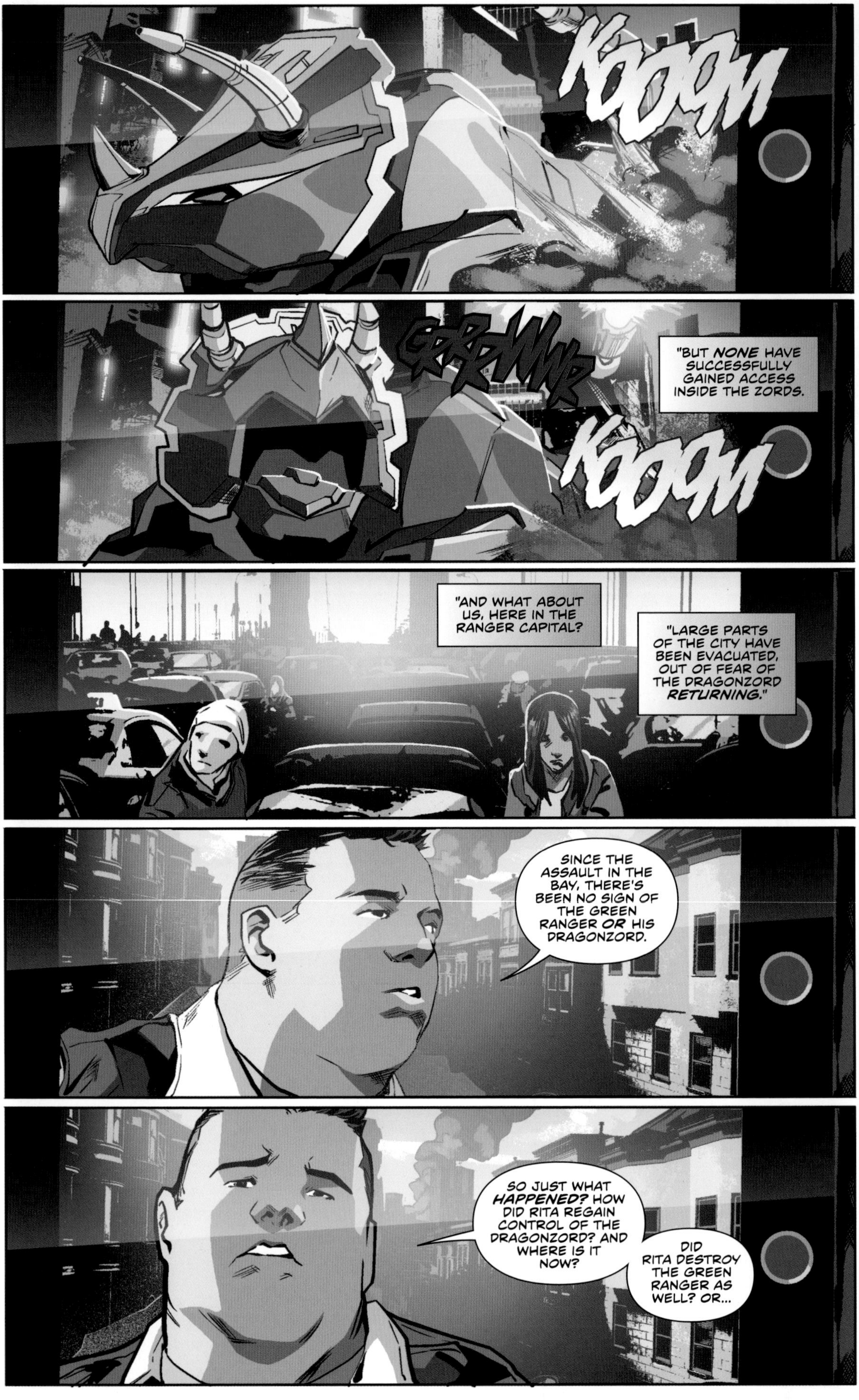
KOOOM
GRRWWR
"BUT NONE HAVE SUCCESSFULLY GAINED ACCESS INSIDE THE ZORDS.
KOOOM
"AND WHAT ABOUT US, HERE IN THE RANGER CAPITAL?
"LARGE PARTS OF THE CITY HAVE BEEN EVACUATED, OUT OF FEAR OF THE DRAGONZORD RETURNING."
SINCE THE ASSAULT IN THE BAY, THERE'S BEEN NO SIGN OF THE GREEN RANGER OR HIS DRAGONZORD.
SO JUST WHAT HAPPENED? HOW DID RITA REGAIN CONTROL OF THE DRAGONZORD? AND WHERE IS IT NOW?
DID RITA DESTROY THE GREEN RANGER AS WELL? OR...

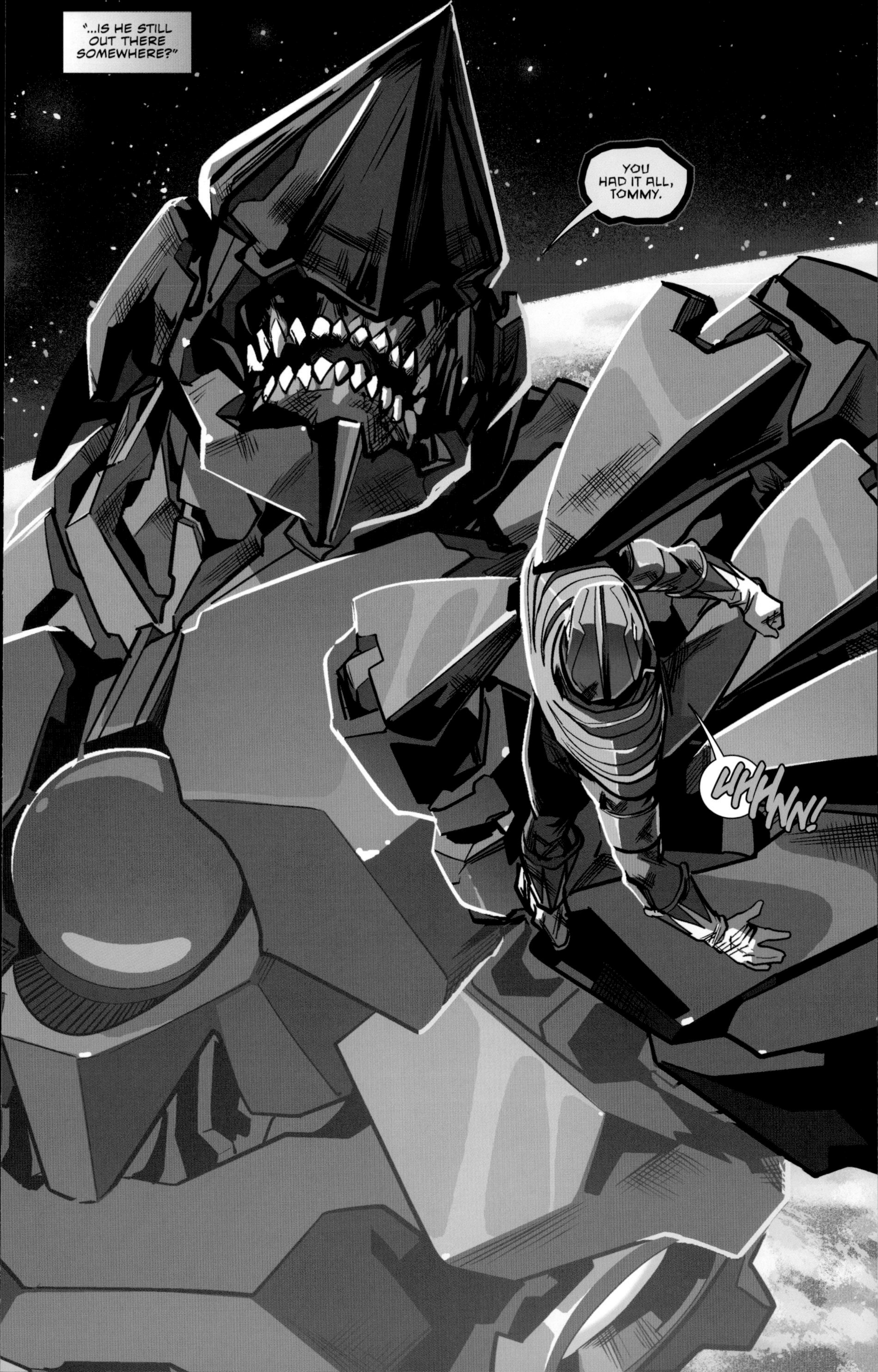
"...IS HE STILL OUT THERE SOMEWHERE?"
YOU HAD IT ALL, TOMMY.
UHHNN!

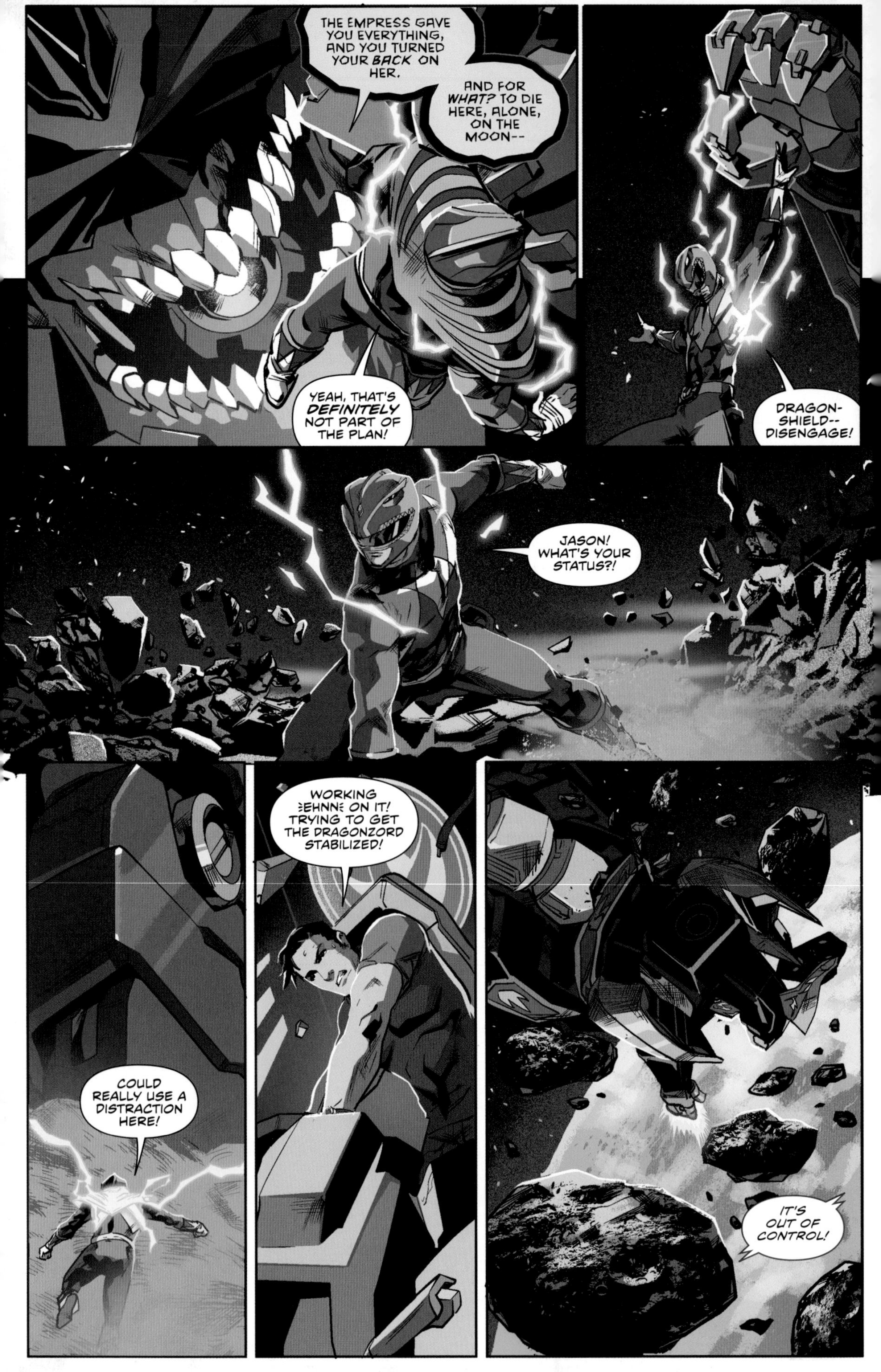
THE EMPRESS GAVE YOU EVERYTHING, AND YOU TURNED YOUR BACK ON HER.
AND FOR WHAT? TO DIE HERE, ALONE, ON THE MOON--
YEAH, THAT'S DEFINITELY NOT PART OF THE PLAN!
DRAGON-SHIELD-- DISENGAGE!
JASON! WHAT'S YOUR STATUS?!
COULD REALLY USE A DISTRACTION HERE!
WORKING EHNN ON IT! TRYING TO GET THE DRAGONZORD STABILIZED!
IT'S OUT OF CONTROL!

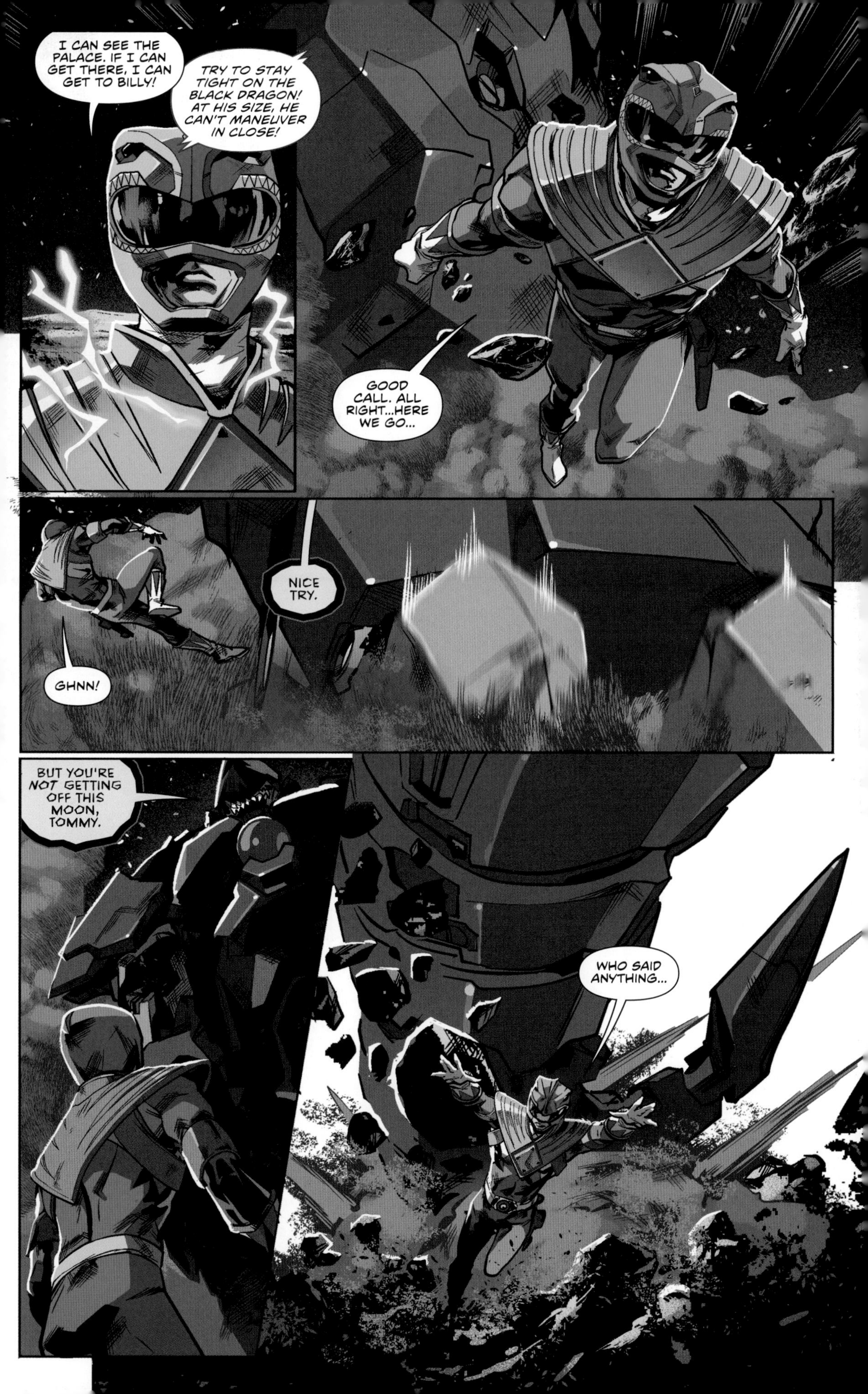
I CAN SEE THE PALACE. IF I CAN GET THERE, I CAN GET TO BILLY!
TRY TO STAY TIGHT ON THE BLACK DRAGON! AT HIS SIZE, HE CAN'T MANEUVER IN CLOSE!
GOOD CALL. ALL RIGHT...HERE WE GO...
NICE TRY.
GHNN!
BUT YOU'RE *NOT* GETTING OFF THIS MOON, TOMMY.
WHO SAID ANYTHING...

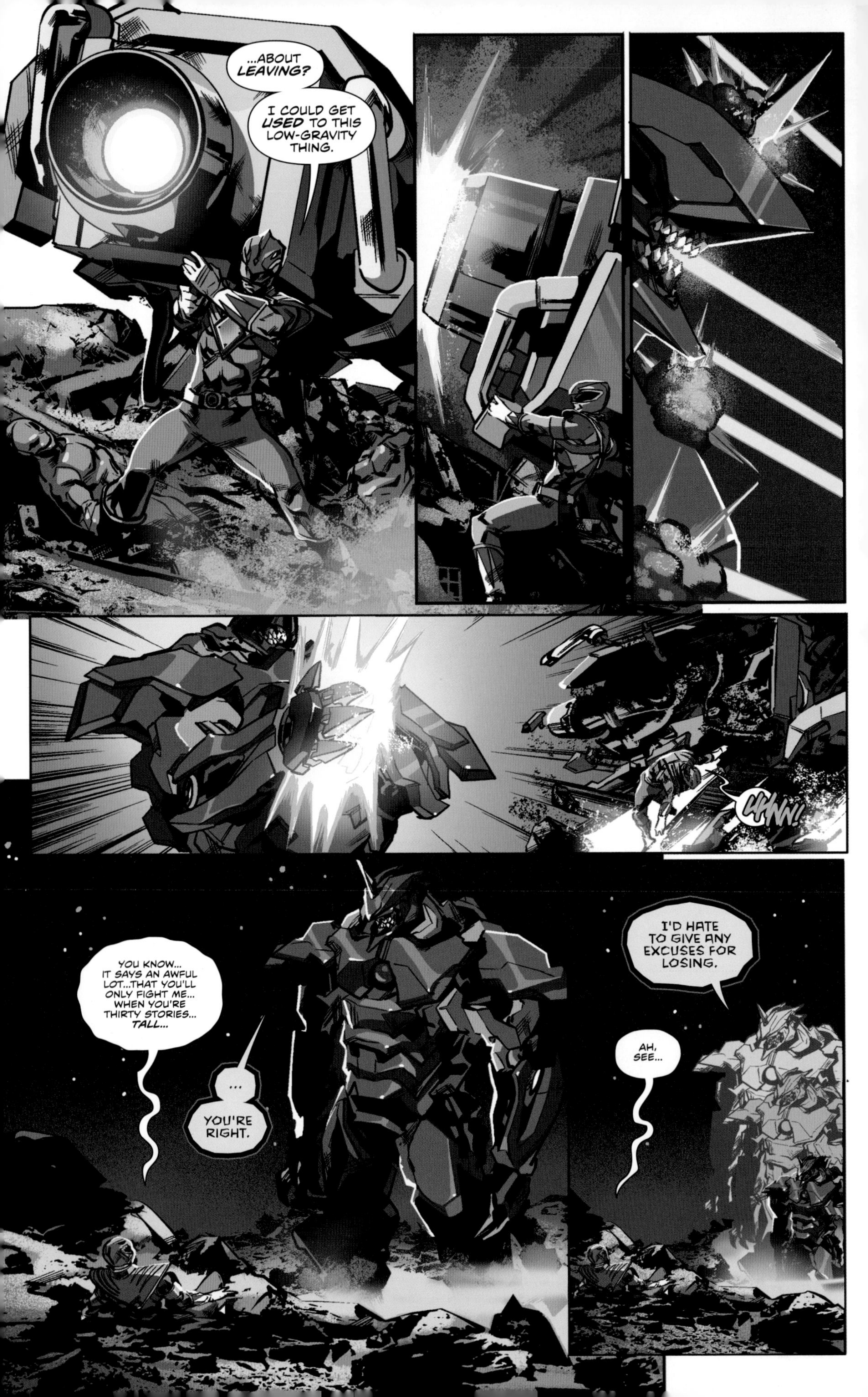
...ABOUT LEAVING?
I COULD GET USED TO THIS LOW-GRAVITY THING.
GNNN!
YOU KNOW... IT SAYS AN AWFUL LOT...THAT YOU'LL ONLY FIGHT ME... WHEN YOU'RE THIRTY STORIES... TALL...
...
YOU'RE RIGHT.
I'D HATE TO GIVE ANY EXCUSES FOR LOSING.
AH, SEE...

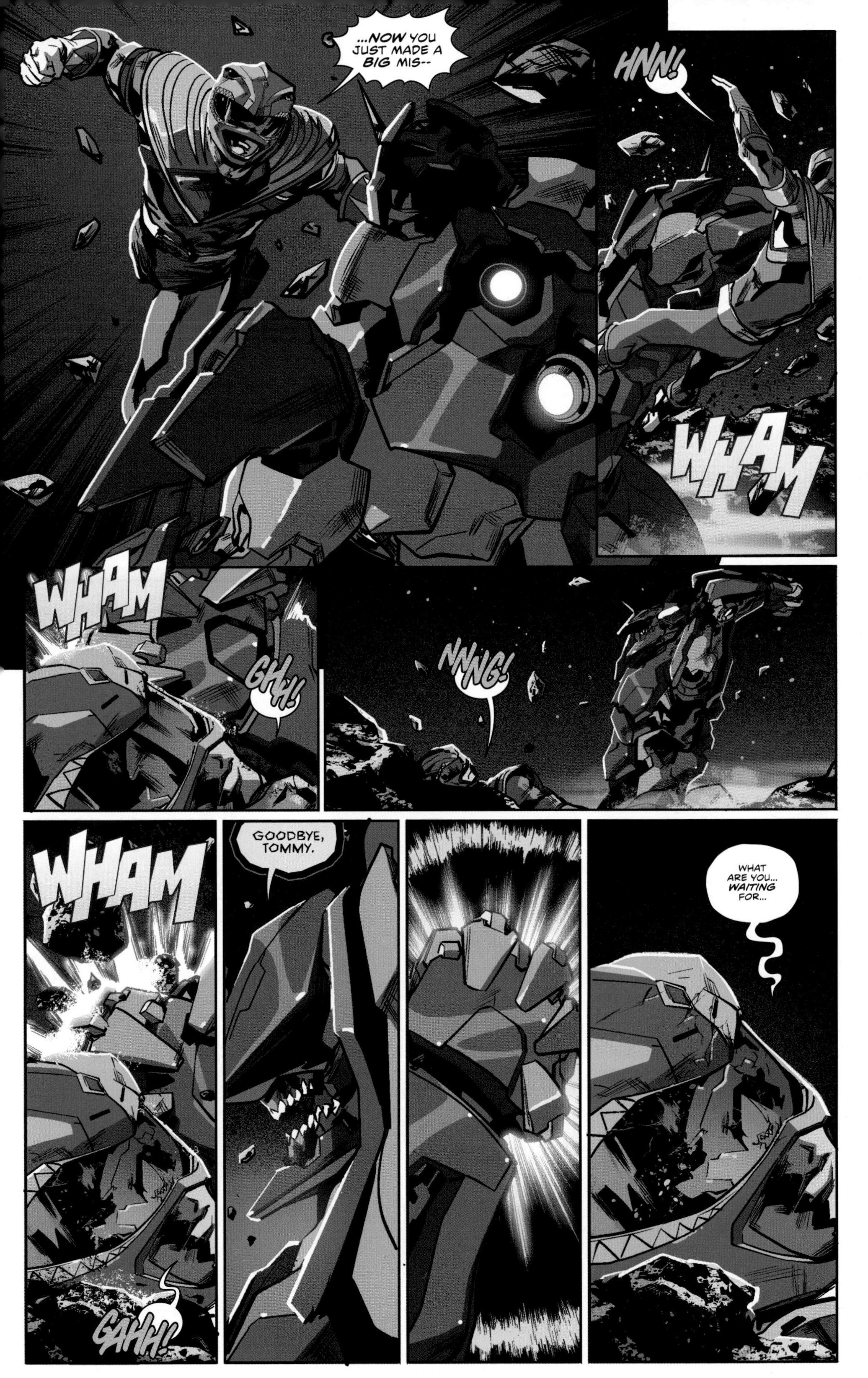

...NOW YOU JUST MADE A BIG MIS--
HNN!
WHAM
WHAM
GHH!
NNNG!
WHAM
GAHH!
GOODBYE, TOMMY.
WHAT ARE YOU... WAITING FOR...

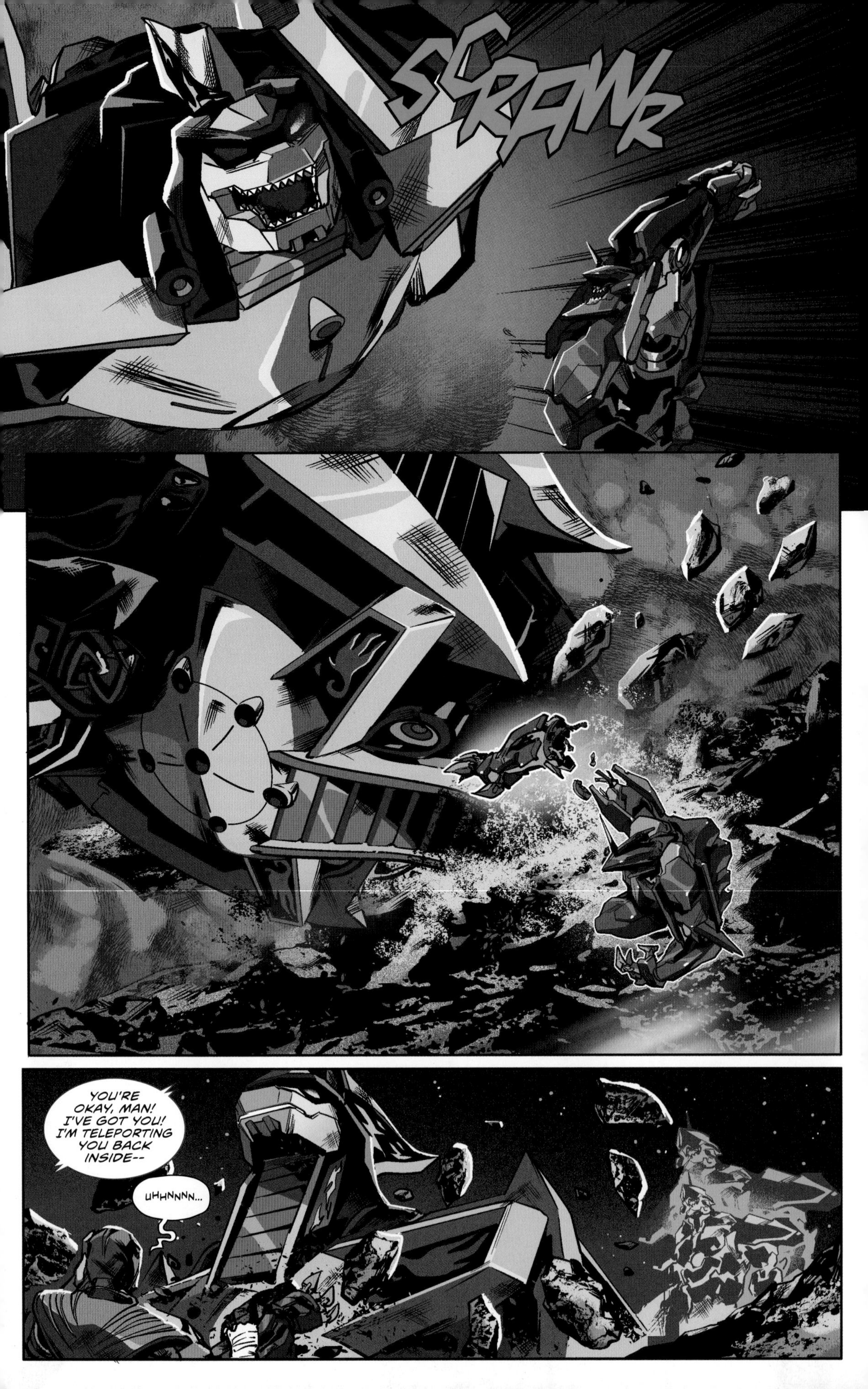
SCRAWR
YOU'RE OKAY, MAN! I'VE GOT YOU! I'M TELEPORTING YOU BACK INSIDE--
UHHNNNN...

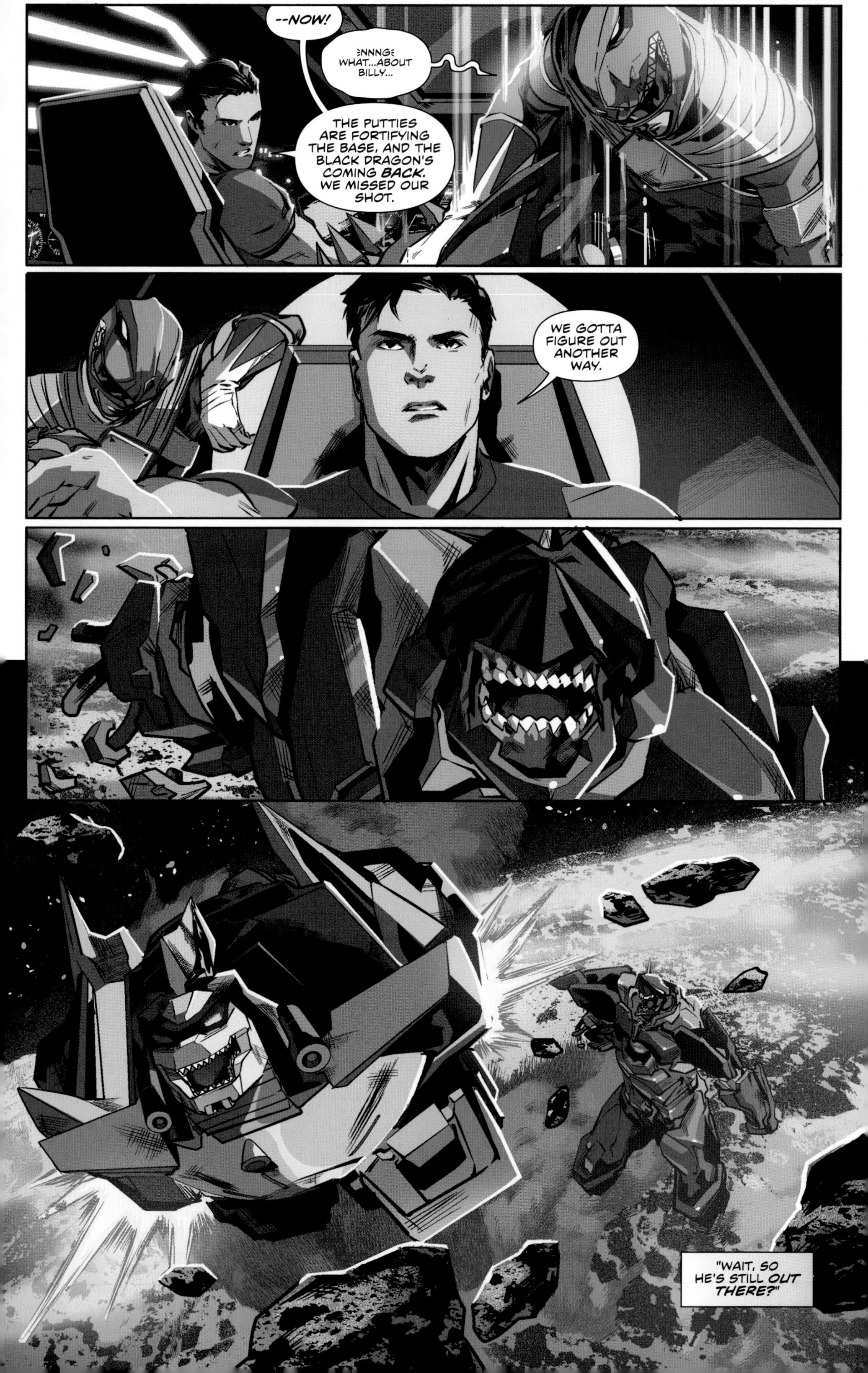
--NOW!
NNNG WHAT...ABOUT BILLY...
THE PUTTIES ARE FORTIFYING THE BASE, AND THE BLACK DRAGON'S COMING BACK. WE MISSED OUR SHOT.
WE GOTTA FIGURE OUT ANOTHER WAY.
"WAIT, SO HE'S STILL OUT THERE?"

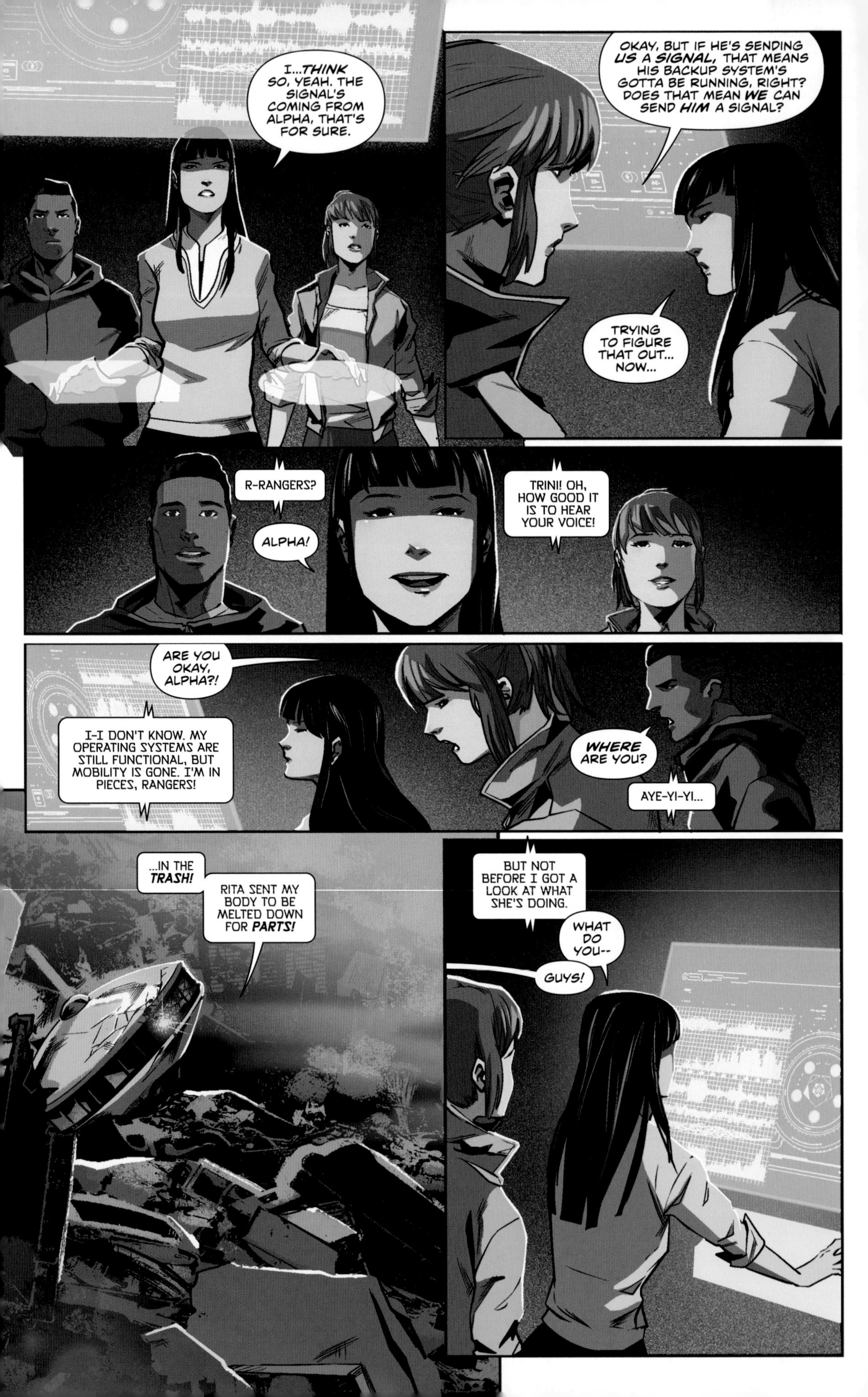
I...THINK SO, YEAH. THE SIGNAL'S COMING FROM ALPHA, THAT'S FOR SURE.
OKAY, BUT IF HE'S SENDING US A SIGNAL, THAT MEANS HIS BACKUP SYSTEM'S GOTTA BE RUNNING, RIGHT? DOES THAT MEAN WE CAN SEND HIM A SIGNAL?
TRYING TO FIGURE THAT OUT... NOW...
R-RANGERS?
ALPHA!
TRINI! OH, HOW GOOD IT IS TO HEAR YOUR VOICE!
ARE YOU OKAY, ALPHA?!
I-I DON'T KNOW. MY OPERATING SYSTEMS ARE STILL FUNCTIONAL, BUT MOBILITY IS GONE. I'M IN PIECES, RANGERS!
WHERE ARE YOU?
AYE-YI-YI...
...IN THE TRASH!
RITA SENT MY BODY TO BE MELTED DOWN FOR PARTS!
BUT NOT BEFORE I GOT A LOOK AT WHAT SHE'S DOING.
WHAT DO YOU--
GUYS!

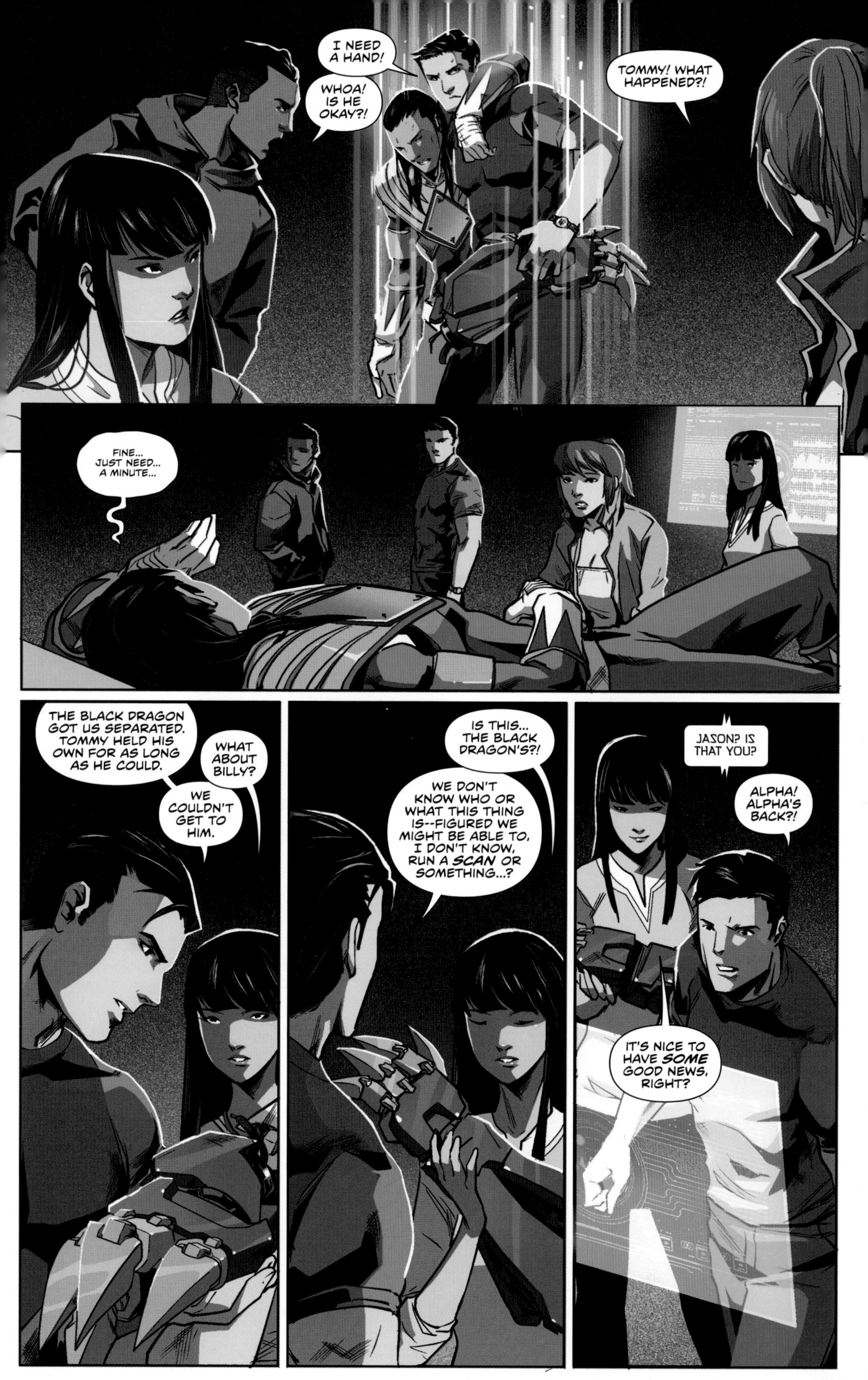
I NEED A HAND!
WHOA! IS HE OKAY?!
TOMMY! WHAT HAPPENED?!
FINE... JUST NEED... A MINUTE...
THE BLACK DRAGON GOT US SEPARATED. TOMMY HELD HIS OWN FOR AS LONG AS HE COULD.
WHAT ABOUT BILLY?
WE COULDN'T GET TO HIM.
IS THIS... THE BLACK DRAGON'S?!
WE DON'T KNOW WHO OR WHAT THIS THING IS--FIGURED WE MIGHT BE ABLE TO, I DON'T KNOW, RUN A SCAN OR SOMETHING...?
JASON? IS THAT YOU?
ALPHA! ALPHA'S BACK?!
IT'S NICE TO HAVE SOME GOOD NEWS, RIGHT?

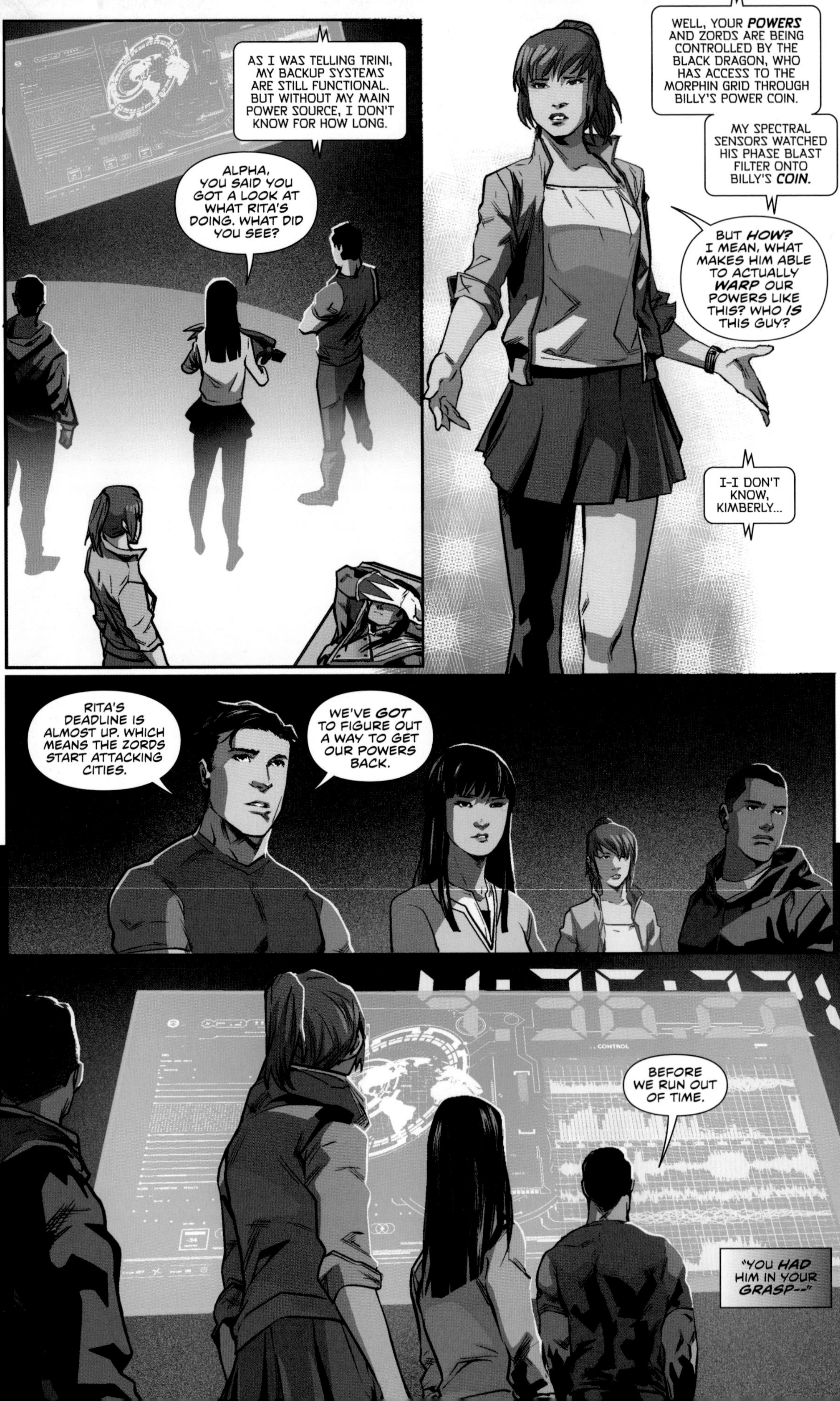
AS I WAS TELLING TRINI, MY BACKUP SYSTEMS ARE STILL FUNCTIONAL. BUT WITHOUT MY MAIN POWER SOURCE, I DON'T KNOW FOR HOW LONG.
ALPHA, YOU SAID YOU GOT A LOOK AT WHAT RITA'S DOING. WHAT DID YOU SEE?
WELL, YOUR POWERS AND ZORDS ARE BEING CONTROLLED BY THE BLACK DRAGON, WHO HAS ACCESS TO THE MORPHIN GRID THROUGH BILLY'S POWER COIN.
MY SPECTRAL SENSORS WATCHED HIS PHASE BLAST FILTER ONTO BILLY'S COIN.
BUT HOW? I MEAN, WHAT MAKES HIM ABLE TO ACTUALLY WARP OUR POWERS LIKE THIS? WHO IS THIS GUY?
I-I DON'T KNOW, KIMBERLY...
RITA'S DEADLINE IS ALMOST UP. WHICH MEANS THE ZORDS START ATTACKING CITIES.
WE'VE GOT TO FIGURE OUT A WAY TO GET OUR POWERS BACK.
CONTROL
BEFORE WE RUN OUT OF TIME.
"YOU HAD HIM IN YOUR GRASP--"

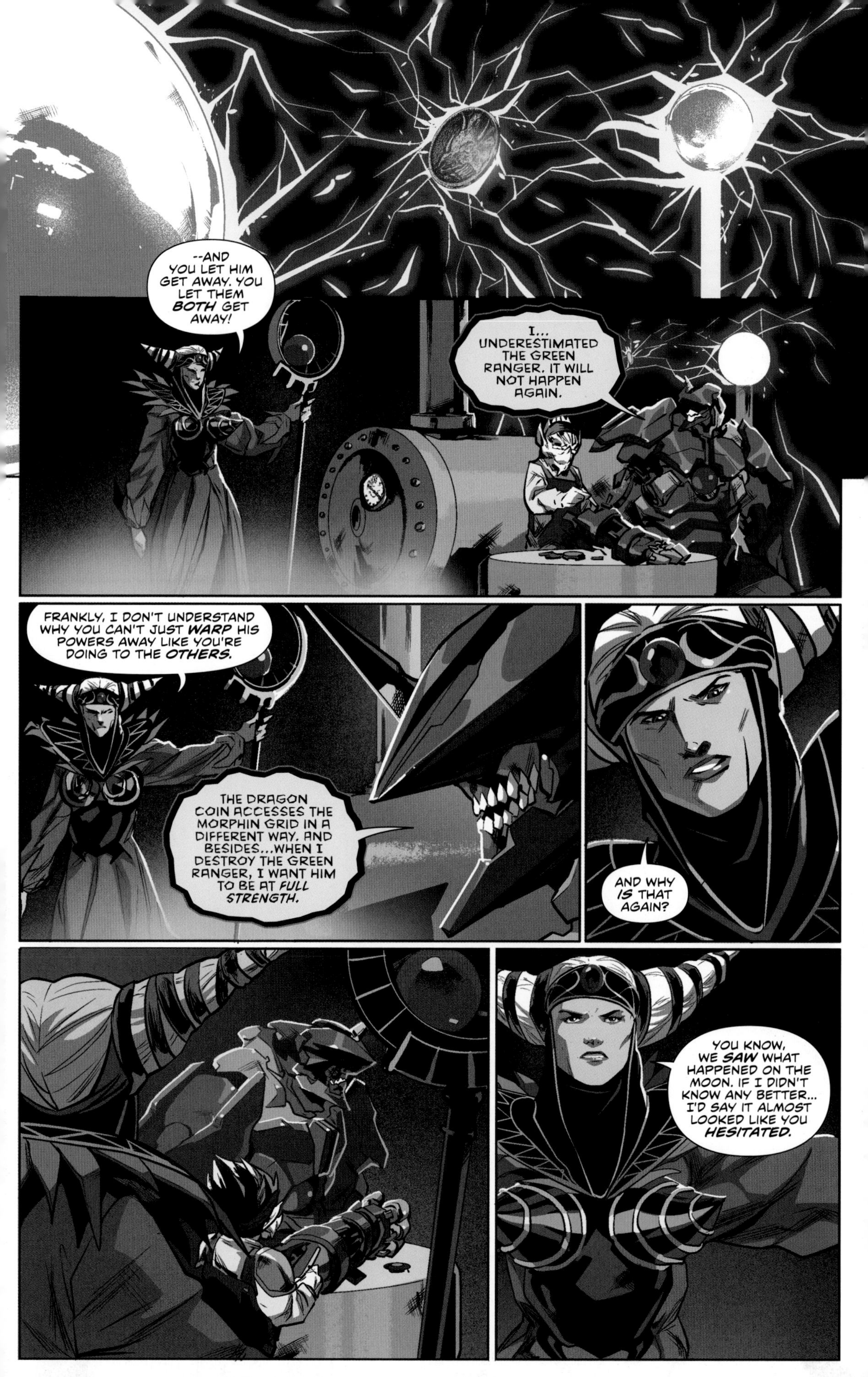
--AND YOU LET HIM GET AWAY. YOU LET THEM BOTH GET AWAY!
I... UNDERESTIMATED THE GREEN RANGER. IT WILL NOT HAPPEN AGAIN.
FRANKLY, I DON'T UNDERSTAND WHY YOU CAN'T JUST WARP HIS POWERS AWAY LIKE YOU'RE DOING TO THE OTHERS.
THE DRAGON COIN ACCESSES THE MORPHIN GRID IN A DIFFERENT WAY. AND BESIDES...WHEN I DESTROY THE GREEN RANGER, I WANT HIM TO BE AT FULL STRENGTH.
AND WHY IS THAT AGAIN?
YOU KNOW, WE SAW WHAT HAPPENED ON THE MOON. IF I DIDN'T KNOW ANY BETTER... I'D SAY IT ALMOST LOOKED LIKE YOU HESITATED.

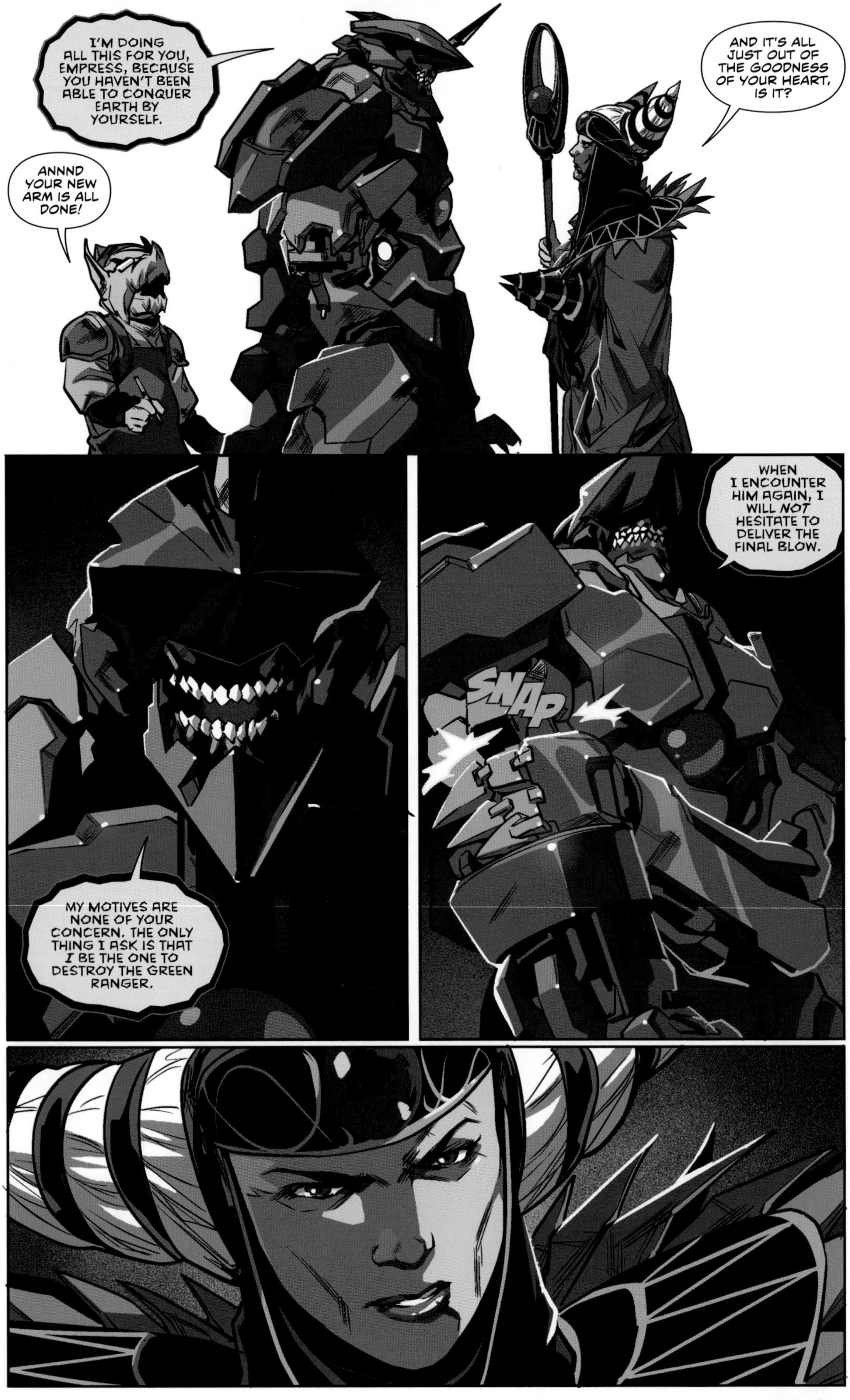
I'M DOING ALL THIS FOR YOU, EMPRESS, BECAUSE YOU HAVEN'T BEEN ABLE TO CONQUER EARTH BY YOURSELF.
AND IT'S ALL JUST OUT OF THE GOODNESS OF YOUR HEART, IS IT?
ANNND YOUR NEW ARM IS ALL DONE!
MY MOTIVES ARE NONE OF YOUR CONCERN. THE ONLY THING I ASK IS THAT *I* BE THE ONE TO DESTROY THE GREEN RANGER.
WHEN I ENCOUNTER HIM AGAIN, I WILL *NOT* HESITATE TO DELIVER THE FINAL BLOW.
SNAP

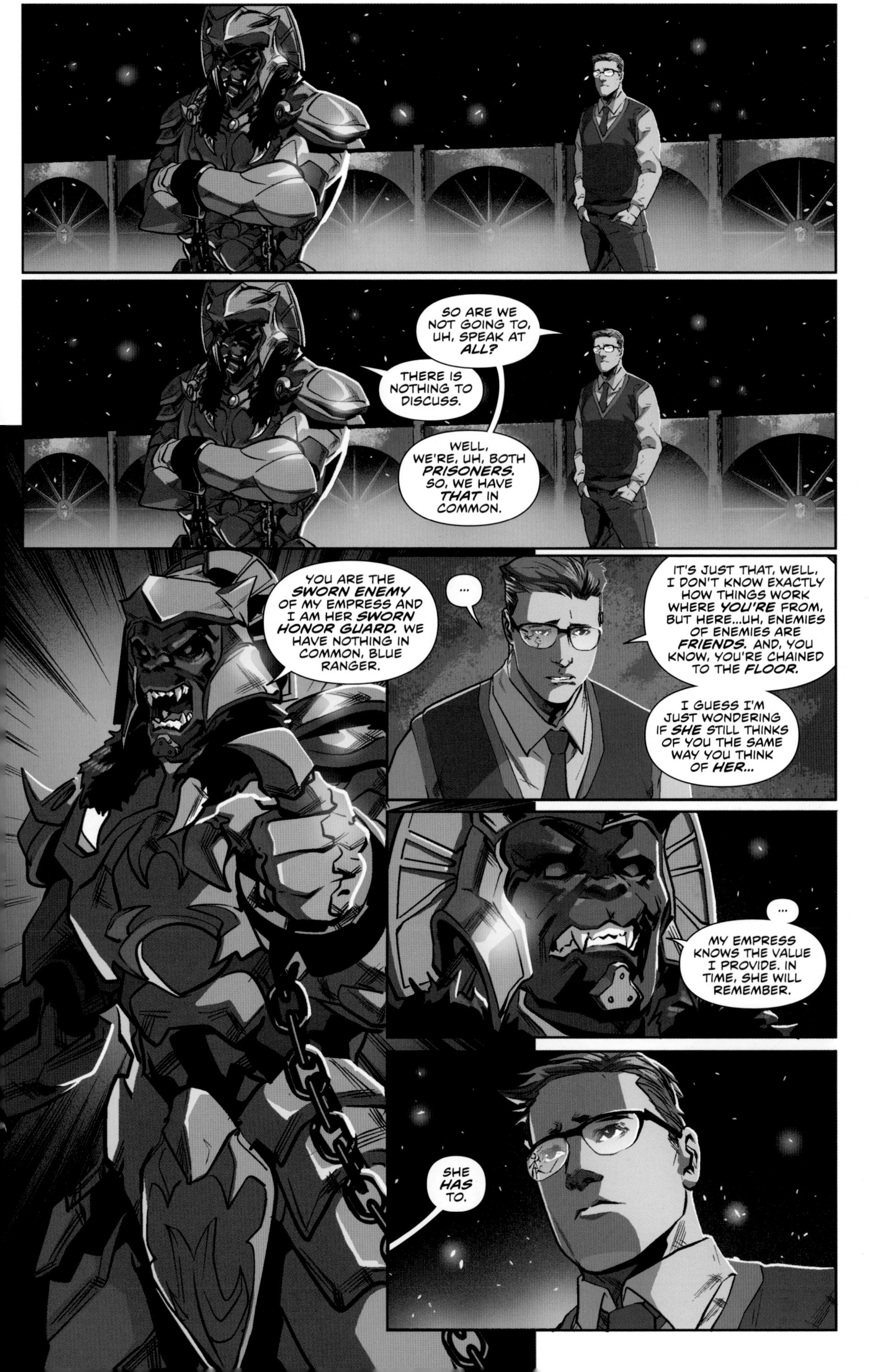
SO ARE WE NOT GOING TO, UH, SPEAK AT ALL?
THERE IS NOTHING TO DISCUSS.
WELL, WE'RE, UH, BOTH PRISONERS. SO, WE HAVE THAT IN COMMON.
YOU ARE THE SWORN ENEMY OF MY EMPRESS AND I AM HER SWORN HONOR GUARD. WE HAVE NOTHING IN COMMON, BLUE RANGER.
...
IT'S JUST THAT, WELL, I DON'T KNOW EXACTLY HOW THINGS WORK WHERE YOU'RE FROM, BUT HERE...UH, ENEMIES OF ENEMIES ARE FRIENDS. AND, YOU KNOW, YOU'RE CHAINED TO THE FLOOR.
I GUESS I'M JUST WONDERING IF SHE STILL THINKS OF YOU THE SAME WAY YOU THINK OF HER...
...
MY EMPRESS KNOWS THE VALUE I PROVIDE. IN TIME, SHE WILL REMEMBER.
SHE HAS TO.

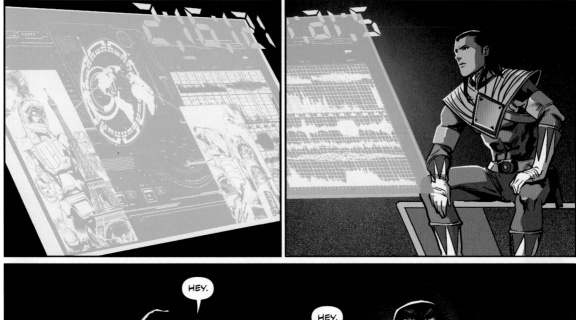

HEY.

HEY.

JASON SAID YOU WENT TOE-TO-TOE WITH THE DRAGON. THE THIRTY-STORIES-TALL VERSION.

I *TRIED* TO.

THAT'S PRETTY RIDICULOUS, MAN.

...YEAH. IN HINDSIGHT, *MAYBE* NOT ONE OF MY BEST IDEAS...

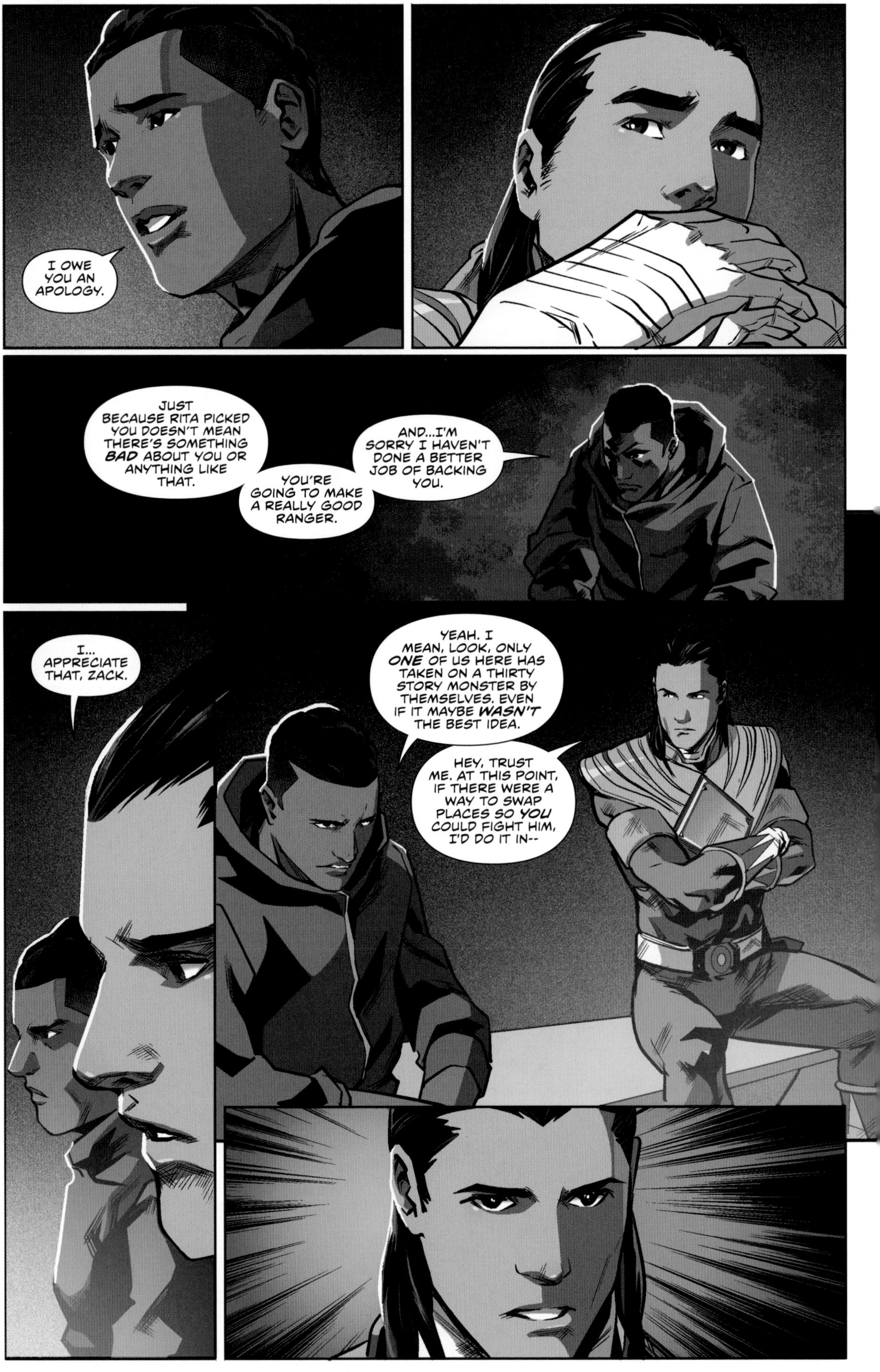
I OWE YOU AN APOLOGY.
JUST BECAUSE RITA PICKED YOU DOESN'T MEAN THERE'S SOMETHING BAD ABOUT YOU OR ANYTHING LIKE THAT.
YOU'RE GOING TO MAKE A REALLY GOOD RANGER.
AND...I'M SORRY I HAVEN'T DONE A BETTER JOB OF BACKING YOU.
I... APPRECIATE THAT, ZACK.
YEAH. I MEAN, LOOK, ONLY ONE OF US HERE HAS TAKEN ON A THIRTY STORY MONSTER BY THEMSELVES. EVEN IF IT MAYBE WASN'T THE BEST IDEA.
HEY, TRUST ME. AT THIS POINT, IF THERE WERE A WAY TO SWAP PLACES SO YOU COULD FIGHT HIM, I'D DO IT IN--

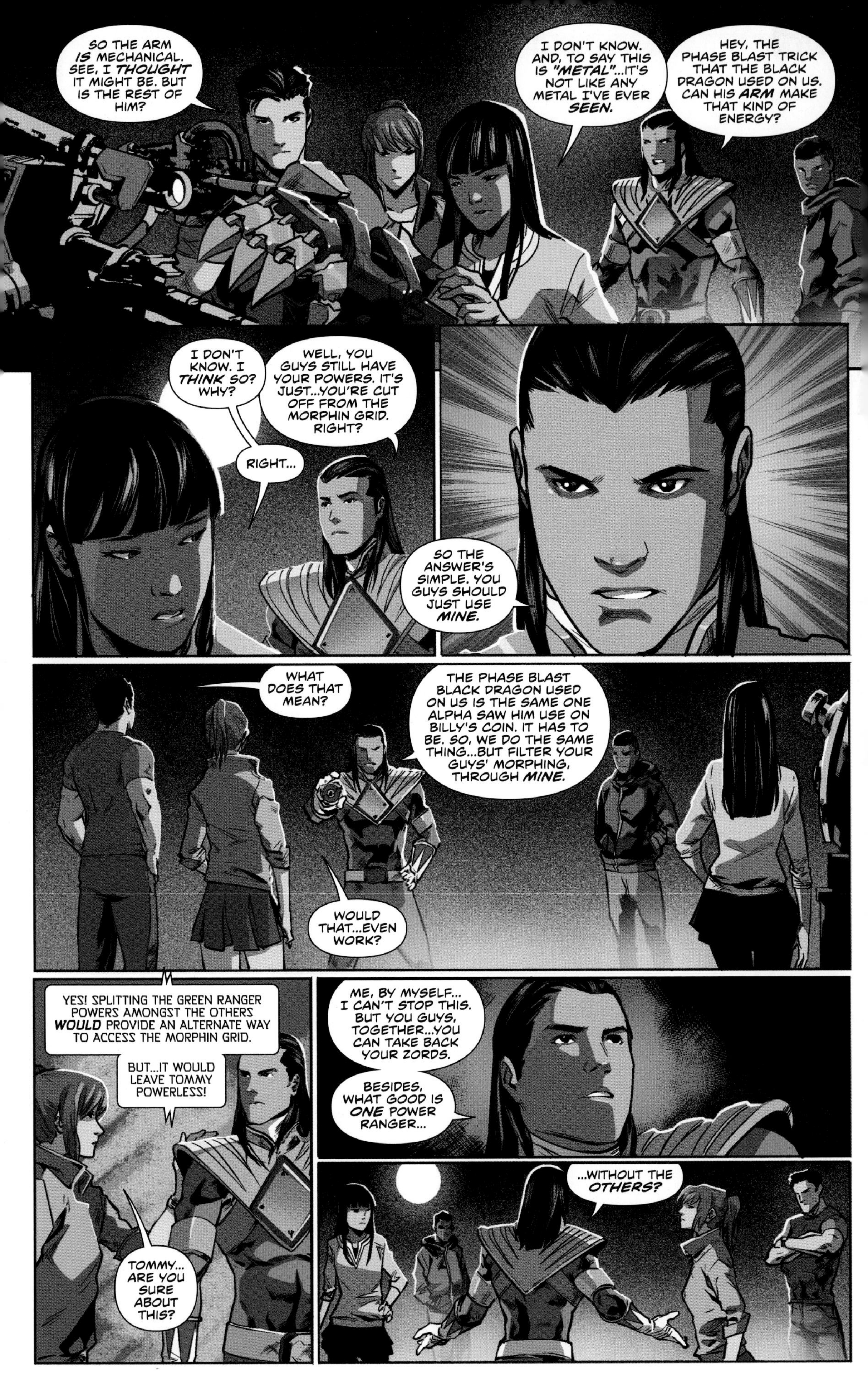
SO THE ARM IS MECHANICAL. SEE, I THOUGHT IT MIGHT BE. BUT IS THE REST OF HIM?
I DON'T KNOW. AND, TO SAY THIS IS "METAL"...IT'S NOT LIKE ANY METAL I'VE EVER SEEN.
HEY, THE PHASE BLAST TRICK THAT THE BLACK DRAGON USED ON US. CAN HIS ARM MAKE THAT KIND OF ENERGY?
I DON'T KNOW. I THINK SO? WHY?
WELL, YOU GUYS STILL HAVE YOUR POWERS. IT'S JUST...YOU'RE CUT OFF FROM THE MORPHIN GRID. RIGHT?
RIGHT...
SO THE ANSWER'S SIMPLE. YOU GUYS SHOULD JUST USE MINE.
WHAT DOES THAT MEAN?
THE PHASE BLAST BLACK DRAGON USED ON US IS THE SAME ONE ALPHA SAW HIM USE ON BILLY'S COIN. IT HAS TO BE. SO, WE DO THE SAME THING...BUT FILTER YOUR GUYS' MORPHING, THROUGH MINE.
WOULD THAT...EVEN WORK?
YES! SPLITTING THE GREEN RANGER POWERS AMONGST THE OTHERS WOULD PROVIDE AN ALTERNATE WAY TO ACCESS THE MORPHIN GRID.
BUT...IT WOULD LEAVE TOMMY POWERLESS!
TOMMY... ARE YOU SURE ABOUT THIS?
ME, BY MYSELF... I CAN'T STOP THIS. BUT YOU GUYS, TOGETHER...YOU CAN TAKE BACK YOUR ZORDS.
BESIDES, WHAT GOOD IS ONE POWER RANGER...
...WITHOUT THE OTHERS?

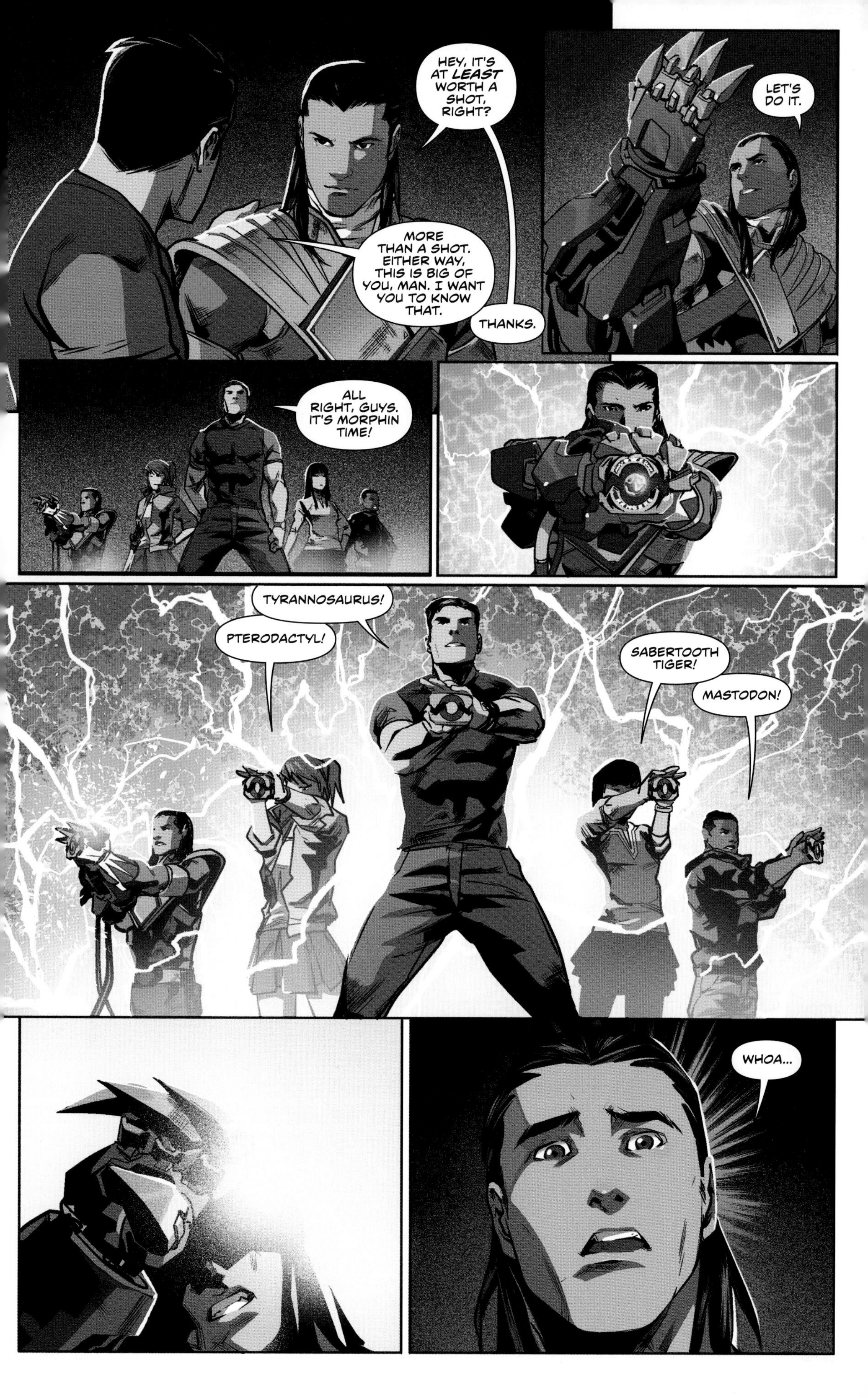
HEY, IT'S AT *LEAST* WORTH A SHOT, RIGHT?
MORE THAN A SHOT. EITHER WAY, THIS IS BIG OF YOU, MAN. I WANT YOU TO KNOW THAT.
THANKS.
LET'S DO IT.
ALL RIGHT, GUYS. IT'S MORPHIN TIME!
TYRANNOSAURUS!
PTERODACTYL!
SABERTOOTH TIGER!
MASTODON!
WHOA...

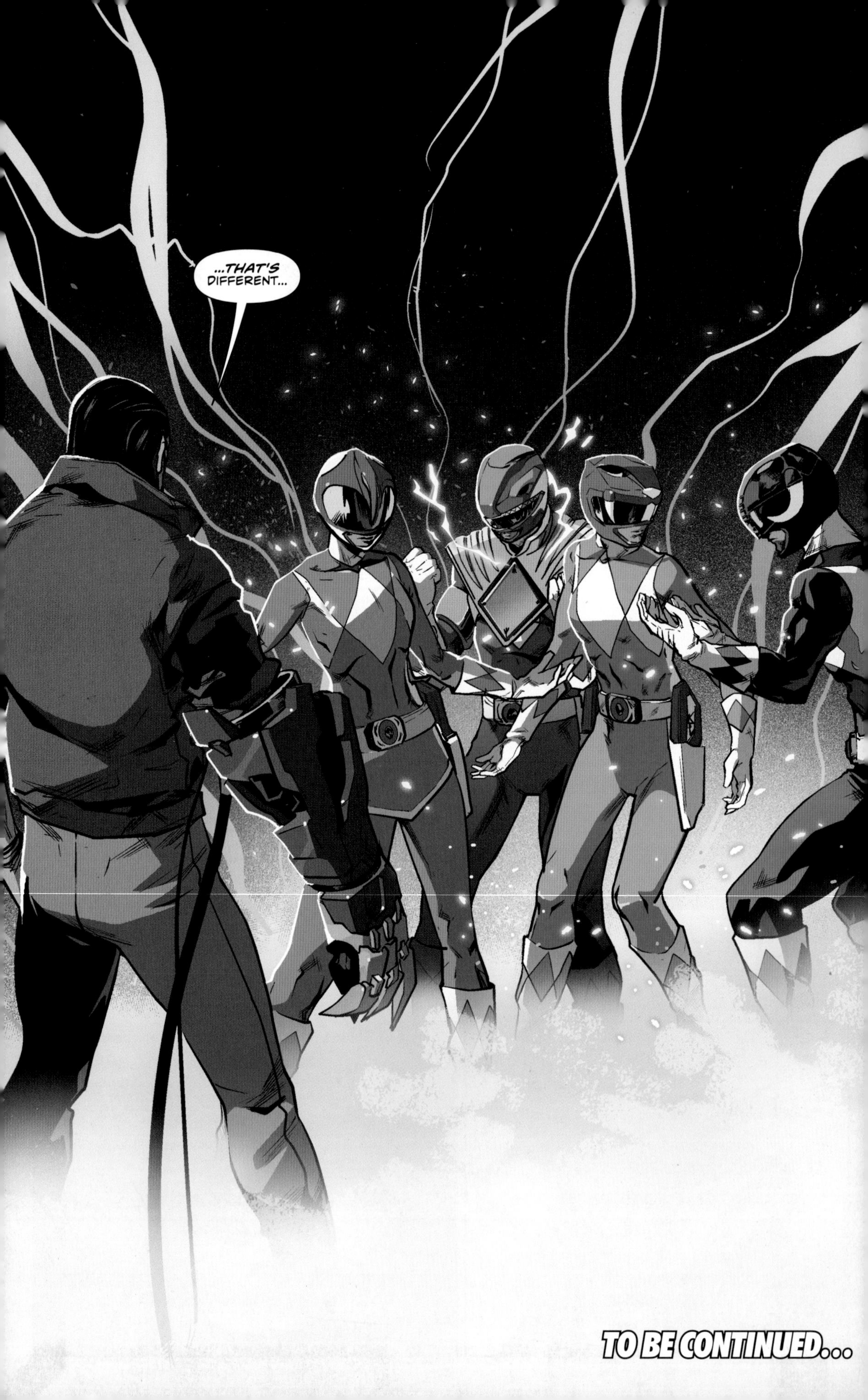
...THAT'S DIFFERENT...
TO BE CONTINUED...

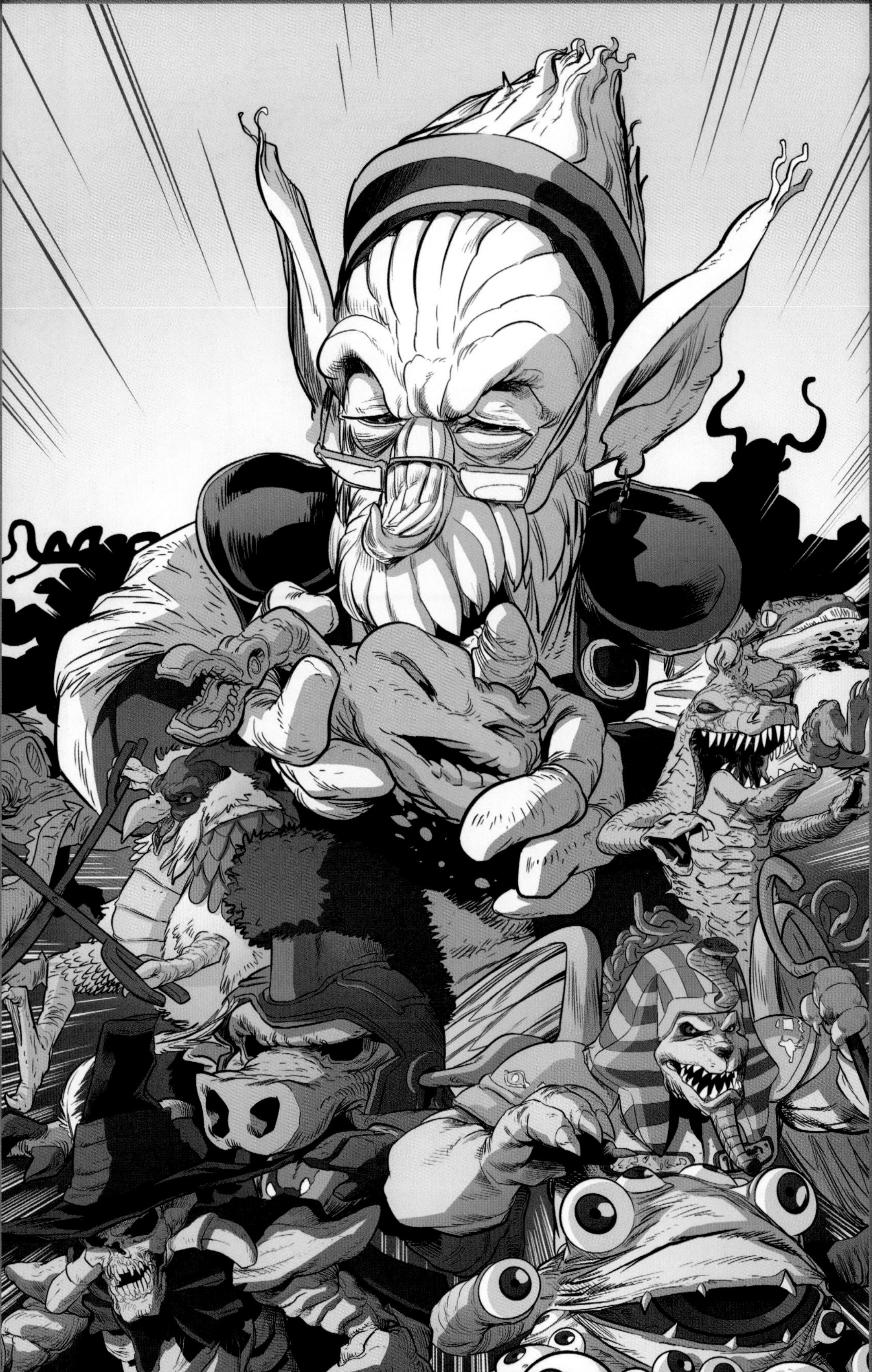

BACHAN WITH COLORS BY **JEREMY LAWSON** VILLAIN VARIANT COVER

SABAN'S

MIGHTY MORPHIN POWER RANGERS

COLLECT THEM ALL!

Set of 9 Hardcover Books ISBN: 978-1-5321-4422-6

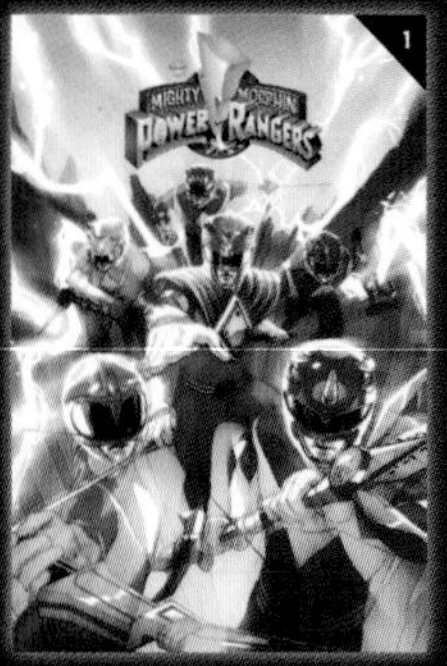

Hardcover Book ISBN 978-1-5321-4423-3

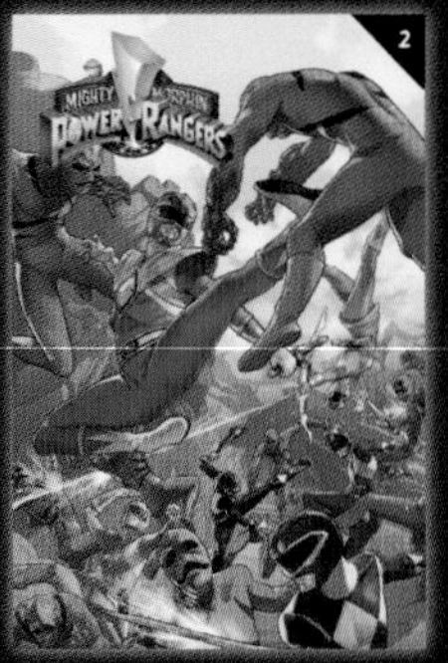

Hardcover Book ISBN 978-1-5321-4424-0

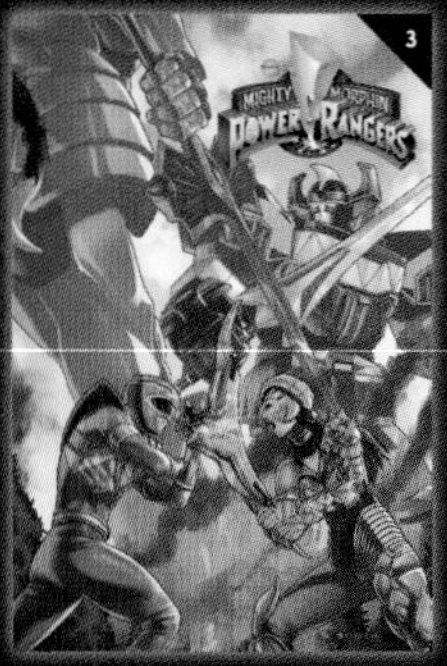

Hardcover Book ISBN 978-1-5321-4425-7

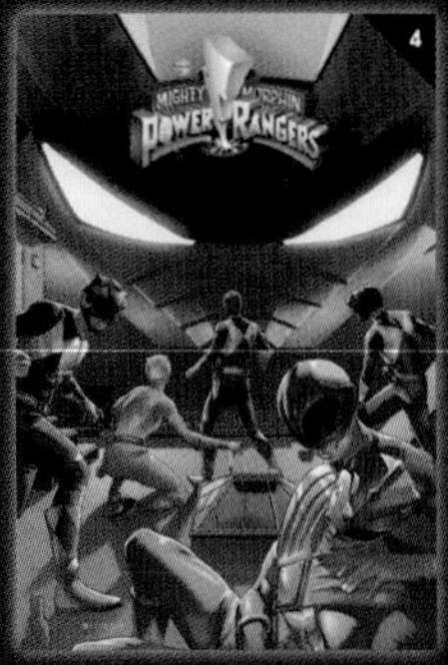

Hardcover Book ISBN 978-1-5321-4426-4

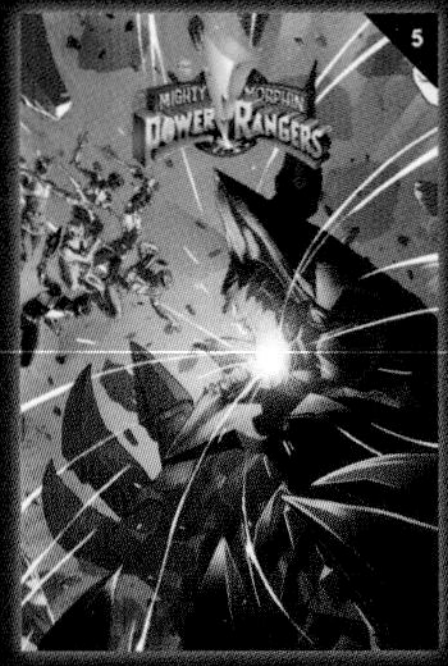

Hardcover Book ISBN 978-1-5321-4427-1

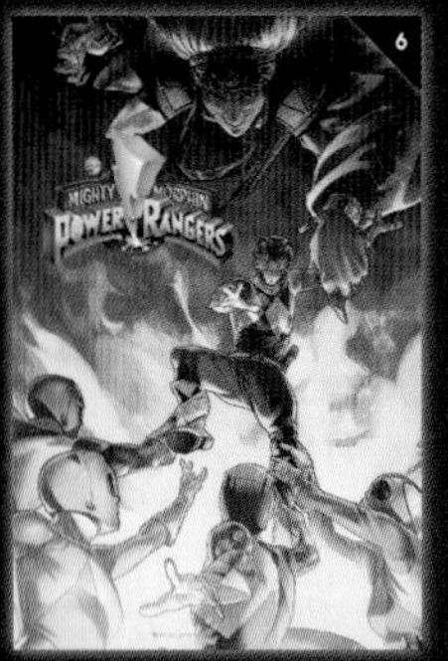

Hardcover Book ISBN 978-1-5321-4428-8

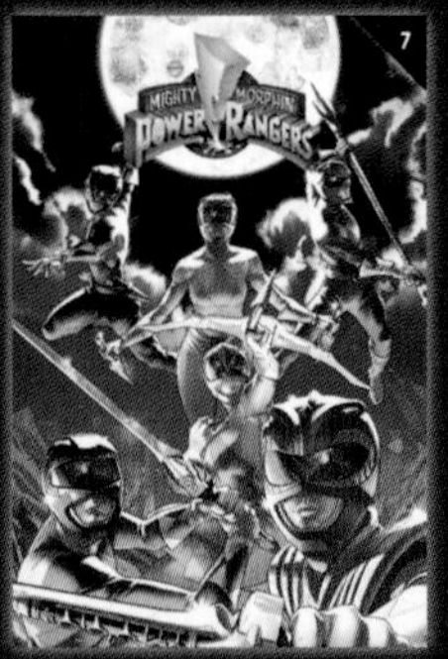

Hardcover Book ISBN 978-1-5321-4429-5

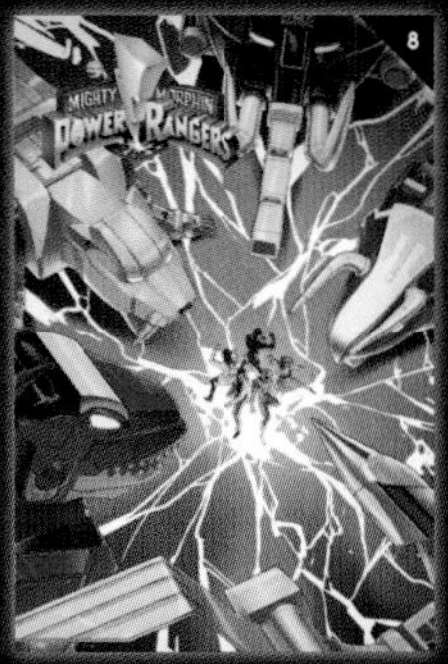

Hardcover Book ISBN 978-1-5321-4430-1

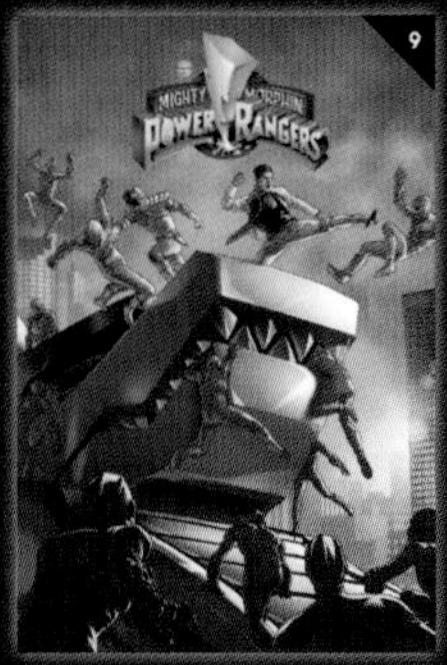

Hardcover Book ISBN 978-1-5321-4431-8